Of Ash and Flames

Cam A. Roze

Published by Cam A. Roze, 2023.

This is a work of fiction. Similarities to real people, places, or events are entirely coincidental.

OF ASH AND FLAMES

First edition. January 16, 2023.

Copyright © 2023 Cam A. Roze.

Written by Cam A. Roze.

Of Ash and Flames

Of Ashes and Flames

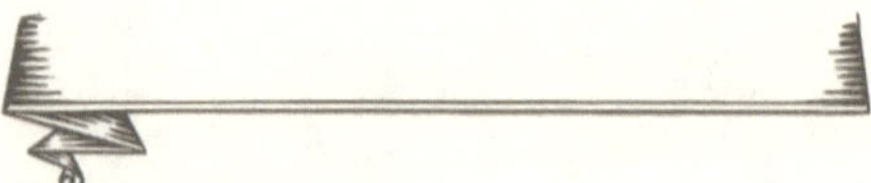

AGE RATING: ALL PUBLIC
Category: Short Story

A small fire genasi experiences life in a very unique way, the other half of her tries to take force, what will become of the Genasi?

Silicia, The Split And An Inferno of Torment

SILICIA, BORN OF TWO fine fire genasi, full of passion. From the elemental tribe of the Southhe tribe had its ways and its wages in wars throughout many of its time and historic teachings. Her father was a tribe warrior who had fought many wars against goblins, orcs, dragonborn and even kobolds.

The tribe had her mother known to be a handy armorer to the tribe, working metals into many sorts. She crafted armors and weapons. She even had made cooking wares of various sorts.

Silicia grew up humbly in this village. She had only begun to walk when the tribe had been invaded. Many speculate the actual events including the lone surviving child. Silicia only would remember the raid to burn the entirety of her home being burnt down to ashes. The screams would always haunt her, although whatever she had seen in that time had been blocked from memory.

Silicia, who'd wandered into the woods and was discovered by a group of elves, was only a small child at the time. The elves decided to try and raise her as one of their kind, seeing as the fire genasi at this time had seemed to vanish from the island.

The elves had taught her many amazing things, like many languages. Her one gift was the library when settled into Inaso, on the far southeast of the island. She knew something was wrong when she hit age five, realizing there were fragmented times happening. She tried to pretend these things were not to occur. Even so the screams from her past would haunt her mind.

The elves had placed her with the orphans. The elves referred to these as the lost ones. Silicia related heavily to the new label, she indeed was lost. Her father and mother to never be seen again. Her mind was fragmented, even beyond her feeling of it.

As the children of the orphanage she shared with them had quickly understood, was that the young girl couldn't handle being around too much water. They would begin to ostracize her for her racial alignment to fire. The genasi was a proud child. The child knew this was a threat to her being. She grew colder as time went forward.

Her head would be hurting constantly and not know why. the time gaps happened more and more often. The children continued to assault her with many insults. She felt darkness within her grow. She tried her best to endure everything she had gone through. At age eight she learned she only could handle so much, awakening the sorceress within her.

One fateful night a short drow of twenty years of age went in to take in a child. He felt the need to share his recent abundance due to his discovery of a map. The drow had deep purple eyes and he seemed to be hypnotic to the people around. She wanted the man to take her. She wanted to learn how to be anted by others, to learn to project a presence like his.

The man was repulsed by her presence in the room. He spat to her. She backed away startled, her hair turned blue from the emotional hurt. The elf panicked and kicked Silicia into the hallway before slamming the door. Her mind began to feel as if it were being sawn in half, only managing to kneel, holding her head. That was the night she can never remember, no matter how hard she would try in coming years. Everyone on the island knows what happened but her on that night. She started to giggle as her head hurt.

"I just wanna play..." Silicia would say muffled from the other side of the door. Her voice almost as deep as a demons.

"But, I like these ones." Silicia would reply in a high pitched whine. "Why do you want to hurt everything?"

"I want the world to be beautiful. Fire is pretty, so let's watch the world burn." Her deepened voice would reply to the higher pitched.

Both voices filled the air for miles. The orphanage was just starting to begin taking everyone outside as quickly as possible. The efforts only saved six individuals that day. Only the sound of the flames would be heard, drowning the sounds of screams that filled the orphanage. Only the walls would be seen, windows with sheer black flames coming out from them. Thick black smokes filled the skies. Silicia, the fire starter that left nothing but rubble and ash surrounding her. No bones were ever discovered so no proper burial ever occurred. She would be on her knees in the rubble.

Silicia would manage her way from her knees holding the right hand side of her face. The little girl walked from the rubble to only see the librarian of the area offer his hand. He seemed unafraid. She was giggling as she approached the elvish librarian. The librarian thought she must have been crying, as a survivor to the tragedy.

"—I'll watch you burn like pretty fire too." Her deeper voice spoke.

"Silicia-" He would try to answer.

"Call me Sil." She would reply as she walked away.

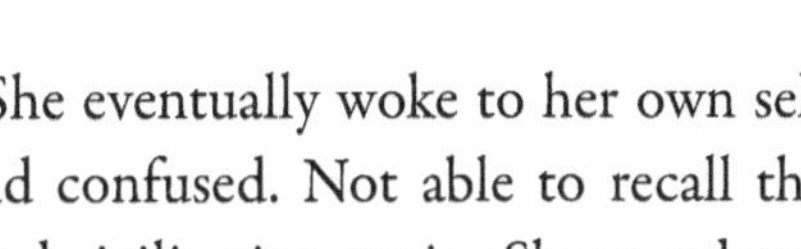

No one followed her. She eventually woke to her own self again, utterly lost and confused. Not able to recall the events, she would aim to find civilization again. She wandered into a deep forest.

She grew quickly being witty in the woods. Silicia, hitting the age of sixteen, had made her own way of surviving in the forest. She had learned of her magic ability as a sorceress and began to constantly push to evolve her knowledge. She had even learned to speak to certain animals. She knew if she had a place to learn and focus, she would be able to have grand ability. She craved that strength of ability. All knowledge was Silicia's goal.

One day, she was headed to the western side of the island, she encountered a strange young girl, who had covered herself in wolves pelts. Silicia had an interest in the seemingly defenseless child. The child, little to Silicia's knowledge, was actually older than herself. The wolf pelt covered one, had been on the run from her pack for some time.

Silicia and the were-being had become quite close as friends in the remaining time in the forest. They had a lot of fun in the woods, although the were-being was not aware. a few weeks had gone by before they even got to know one anothers names. the were-being was names Athii, as she had been raised in the woods by her old pack, where she was supposed to be the next in line for being the alpha female. Athii had no interest in such ideas.

Silicia and Athii relocated to the far west of the island. Silicia helped Athii build her home north to Ostros. Silicia wished Athii the best, hoping they would meet again one day.

Silicia decided she would go onward in life by adventuring for her means of living. She longed to belong somewhere, any-where, so long as she would fit in. Somewhere people would like her. She went forth on her adventures to fulfill the longing with-in the void left in her heart. She went to Ostros, a city of giants, to discover the tieflings, a divine race as she came to understand.

She stayed with them for a while to learn the language of In-fernal. She also went forward to study the language of the giants. She hoped to gain their trust and asked to settle with them, to only get rejected by the settlement. She took that as she was only being sent onward to complete more work.

She left the large settlement for a place named Boulders Gates, where the races were very mixed. No one hardly took notice of her appearance or race. It seemed everyone here had a place to belong. She was eager to see all this city had to offer. She had hoped that she finally found the place that she belonged.

She stayed in a tavern ran by an old fire Genasi, named Eladorn within the city walls. She had explained everything as she recalled it to the fire genasi, hoping for once that she would find someone who understood. He admittedly didn't relate. Even so, he hired her to be his barkeep. She liked this idea. During the time she worked with Eladorn, she had made the establishment stand out. Most of the time people would be disregarding the warm ales as they got in their service at the tavern.

Eladorn had taken notice, the young Gensai, Silicia had no idea how to fix this issue. No one wanted warm ale but, most were too polite to mention such a thing to Silicia. Eladorn himself being a sorcerer of sorts, took the time to teach Silicia a spell known as 'Ice Knife' which she had started to utilize to keep the ale fresh and cool. They had a ton of grand success in this endeavor, fixing the only issue the tavern had.

Silicia had learned how to prepare many foods with her natural elemental alignment. Eladorn took pride in teaching the younger fire genasi. He knew she had a lot of potential and power tucked away within. he could sense the darkness of her heart still present even with the time passed by. He trusted her, none the less.

Eladorn after five years of successfully teaching Silicia. On the day that they claimed her birthday to be, he gave her the deed to the tavern. The Dragons Tankard would be hers for as long as she had decided so. Eladorn explained he would be back again one day, however, it would not to be her aid, but to ask for it instead.

They spent the entire day celebrating with some of the locals. A small knit community was beginning to form, she was becoming a bit of an icon in the community. Everyone had a reason to adore Silicia, whether it was from service at the tavern, or simply understanding the other people in the community. She felt valued. She felt she belonged. Silicia earned her place in Boulders Gates. She went to bed early that night in a drunken bliss.

Eladorn disappeared that night, leaving Silicia to the tavern. The tavern ran smoothly for a week. She had everyone satisfied with her services, even to the point she had started to save enough gold for an addition to the tavern. She wanted to offer an inn for passersby. Surely this would be welcome to offer travelers a place to stay.

Then one fateful day, a young drow entered the tavern with a water genasi, claiming they were the heroes of this island.

The drow had a faintly memorable feature, deep purple eyes. Silicia knew better. Eladorn would have been a true hero in her mind. She could feel a pulse wash over her, to no effect on her.

"So, where's Eladorn?" The drow asked Silicia.

"He no longer owns the establishment." She would reply quietly.

"So then who owns it?" The drow asked her, the water genasi keeping a hand on the drows shoulder.

"I own this place now." Silicia said.

"Where did Eladorn go?" The drow spoke with haste. aggression was tense in his voice.

"He's resuming his adventuring." Silicia would say.

"You killed him didn't you? For the deed?" The drow spoke.

"Thats rude..." The water genasi interjeted.

"I.. did... no... such.. thing..." Silicia's breathing got heavy.

"Oh, push a button did I?" The drow would taunt.

"Fire..." Silicia mumbled as she gripped her head.

"Miss... are you okay?" The water genasi would try to check on Silicia.

Within the blink of an eye Silicia bursts into an inferno of black flames. Her eyes faded into jet black like coals. She grabbed the water genasi by the shirt and threw her through the front door, off the doors hinges The genasi ended up in the cobblestone streets, laying on their back, hardly breathing.

"You're gonna regret that, girl." The drow growled at Silicia. The tavern slowly emptied until it was just them in the dining area.

"No, I am gonna make you pretty like fire." Silicia said with a smile, the voice drop happening yet again. This time, she didn't even get a hint that she was losing herself.

The drow drew their blade. Just as quick as they drew it Silicia had her hands over the sword. She smiled at the drow, his panic beginning to set in. His eyes flashed a purple color into her eyes, besides just causing her to get irritated, it had not effect. The drow wore an expression of sheer disbelief.

She twisted her hands and snapped the heated blade from her touch. Never had the drow experienced such terror. She laid a hand on the drow's cheek, kissing him gently, as he tried to scream from the burning she ensued on his body. She let her kiss go, the drows body dropped to the floor. Smoke raised from the seared body of the drow. Silicia believed the drow to be dead.

Silicia dragged out the body into the street for the water genasi to dispose of. She smiled to the water genasi. The water genasi was frozen in terror. She ran off to hide, not to be heard of for many years to come. The water genasi will never forget the events she encountered with Silicia that fateful day.

Silicia's reputation as twin spirited was rampid and spreading all over the island. Many would travel to her tavern for business. Many would request to be her apprentice in many of her crafts. She was a wise genasi, however, there was a part of Silicia everyone knew to get away from.

The locals help Silicia on a regular basis now, her being a vital cornerstone to the community. They all have come to adore her. When she splits now, they help her rebuild the tragic losses. They know she always means the best. Most have learned now just what to avoid talking about near her.

Silicia, from ash and flame, traveled through hells beyond the typical. She gained her respect by becoming a barmaid. Then a proprietor, none the less.Who ever would have thought a bar was the best place for a fire genasi.

Don't miss out!

Visit the website below and you can sign up to receive emails whenever Cam A. Roze publishes a new book. There's no charge and no obligation.

https://books2read.com/r/B-A-CUFV-CAPEC

BOOKS 2 READ

Connecting independent readers to independent writers.

About the Author

Cam A. Roze is a Dark Fantasy Author. they strive to have immersive worlds and rich lore in all of their endeavors

www.ingramcontent.com/pod-product-compliance
Lightning Source LLC
Chambersburg PA
CBHW021130070726

47591CB00014B/2246